This book must be returned by the date specified at the time of issue as
the DUE DATE FOR RETURN

The loan may be extended (personally, by post, telephone or online) for
a further period, if the book is not required by another reader, by quoting
the barcode / author / title.

Enquiries: 01709 336774

www.rotherham.gov.uk/libraries

The Little Red Hen

Susanna Davidson

Illustrated by
Daniel Postgate

Reading Consultant: Alison Kelly
Roehampton University

Map of the farm

Farmhouse

Hen house

Duck pond

Barn

N
W · E
S

Field

Mill

Bakehouse

Once upon a time,
there was a
little red hen.

She lived on a farm in a
little white hen house
with a bright red roof.

5

The little red hen had
three best friends.

Good morning,
black cat.

A glossy
black cat

Meeeow!

who lived in the
farmhouse.

A big noisy duck who
lived on the pond.

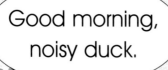

8

And a fat brown rat
who lived in the barn.

One morning, the little red hen walked to the field.

Hide! It's the little red hen.

She was looking for juicy worms to eat.

10

She went scratch,
scratch,
scratch

with her small sharp toes

and she found some
grains of wheat.

11

"Ooh!" she cried. She fluffed her feathers.

"Cluck, cluck, cluck!"

"Who will help me plant the wheat?"

"Not I," said the cat.

"Not I," said the duck.

"Not I," said the rat.

"Fine!" said the little red hen. "Then I'll do it myself."

And she did.

The little red hen pecked at the ground and made a hole.

What a waste of time.

One by one,
she dropped
the grains in.

The little red hen waited
for her wheat to grow
all through the
winter.

First, the shoots were
small and green.

18

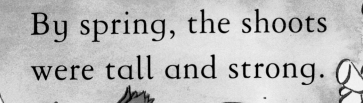

By spring, the shoots
were tall and strong.

In summer, they
turned from
green to gold.

At last, the wheat
was ready.

"Who will
help me cut it
down?" said the
little red hen.

"Not I," said the cat.

"Not I," said the duck.

"Not I," said the rat.

"Fine!" said the little red hen. "Then I'll cut it down myself."

And she did.

She cut down the
wheat without
any help at all.

"Who will help me take the wheat to the mill?" said the little red hen.

"I want to grind it into flour."

"Not I," said
the cat.

"Not I,"
said the duck.

27

"Not I," said the rat.

"Fine!" said
the little red hen.
"Then I'll take it to
the mill myself!"

And she did.

She took the wheat
to the mill

and ground it into flour,
without any help at all.

"Who will help me make the flour into bread?" said the little red hen.

"Not I," said the cat.

"Not I," said the duck.

"Not I," said the rat.

"Then I'll make it myself," said the little red hen.

And she did.

She baked the bread
without any help at all.

"Who will help me eat the bread?" said the little red hen.

The cat, the duck and
the rat jumped up.

"Mmm," they said, as they smelled the bread.

The bread was warm and soft.

"I'll eat the bread,"
said the cat.

"I'll eat the bread," said the duck.

"I'll eat the bread,"
said the rat.

"Oh no you won't!"
said the little red hen.

"I'll eat it ALL BY
MYSELF!"

And she did.

The little red hen's guide to making bread

First she gets:
450g (1lb) (3½ cups) strong white
bread flour
½ teaspoon salt
½ teaspoon sugar
2 teaspoons dried easy-blend yeast
or 1 teaspoon dried rapid rise yeast
300ml (1 cup) warm water
2 tablespoons olive or vegetable oil

When the little red hen reaches step
8, she heats her oven to 220°C,
425°F, gas mark 7.

1. First, she sifts
the flour, sugar
and salt through
a sieve into a large
bowl. Then, she
stirs in the yeast.

2. The little red hen
then mixes the
water and oil. Next,
she pours them into
a hollow in the
middle of the flour.

3. She uses a
wooden spoon to
mix everything
together until
she's made a
soft dough.

4. Then, she
puts the dough
onto a floury
work surface
and kneads it
for 10 minutes.

5. Next, the little red hen puts the dough into a clean bowl and covers it with plastic foodwrap.

6. She leaves the bowl in a warm place for 1½ hours. The dough rises to twice its size.

7. She kneads the dough for a minute to get rid of any air bubbles. Then, she puts the dough in a buttered loaf tin.

8. The little red hen leaves the dough for an hour in a warm place. Meanwhile, she turns on her oven.

9. She puts her loaf on the middle oven shelf and leaves it to bake for 35-40 minutes.

10. She leaves it to cool on a wire rack. Then she eats it all by herself!

Ask an adult to help you!

The Little Red Hen is an old, old folk tale.
It has been around for hundreds of years.
No one knows who first told it, but it
probably came from Russia.

Series editor: Lesley Sims
Designed by Louise Flutter
Cover design by Russell Punter

The right of Daniel Postgate to be identified as the illustrator of this
Work has been asserted by him in accordance with the Copyright
Designs and Patents Act 1988.

First published in 2006 by Usborne Publishing Ltd., Usborne House,
83-85 Saffron Hill, London EC1N 8RT, England. www.usborne.com
Copyright © 2006 Usborne Publishing Ltd.

48